Bill and Ben

In these stories you will meet:

Bill and Ben

The Fat Controller

Jack

Thomas

Ned

And these more difficult words:
listen   fast

EGMONT

We bring stories to life

Book Band: Yellow

First published in Great Britain in 2016 by Egmont UK Limited,
The Yellow Building, 1 Nicholas Road, London W11 4AN

Thomas the Tank Engine & Friends ™

CREATED BY BRITT ALLCROFT

Based on the Railway Series by the Reverend W Awdry
© 2016 Gullane (Thomas) LLC. Thomas the Tank Engine & Friends and
Thomas & Friends are trademarks of Gullane (Thomas) Limited.
Thomas the Tank Engine & Friends and Design is Reg. U.S. Pat. & Tm. Off.
© 2016 HIT Entertainment Limited.

HiT entertainment

ISBN 978 1 4052 8260 4

63404/1

Printed in Singapore

Stay safe online. Egmont is not responsible
for content hosted by third parties.

Series and book banding consultant: Nikki Gamble

Bill and Ben

This is Bill.

This is Ben.

Bill was at the pit.

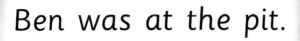

Ben was at the pit.

The Fat Controller
had a big job for
Bill and Ben.

Bill and Ben had trucks to pull.

The trucks were bad.
The trucks did not
listen to Bill and Ben.

The Fat Controller was cross.

You did not do the big job, Bill and Ben. Go back to the pit.

At the pit Bill and Ben
were sad.

BRENDAM BAY

Crash!
What was that?

Rocks fell. **Crash!** The men got in Bill and Ben's trucks.

Lots of rocks fell.
Crash!

Bill and Ben
went fast.

Bill and Ben did a good job.

Jack the Digger

This is Jack.
Jack is a digger.

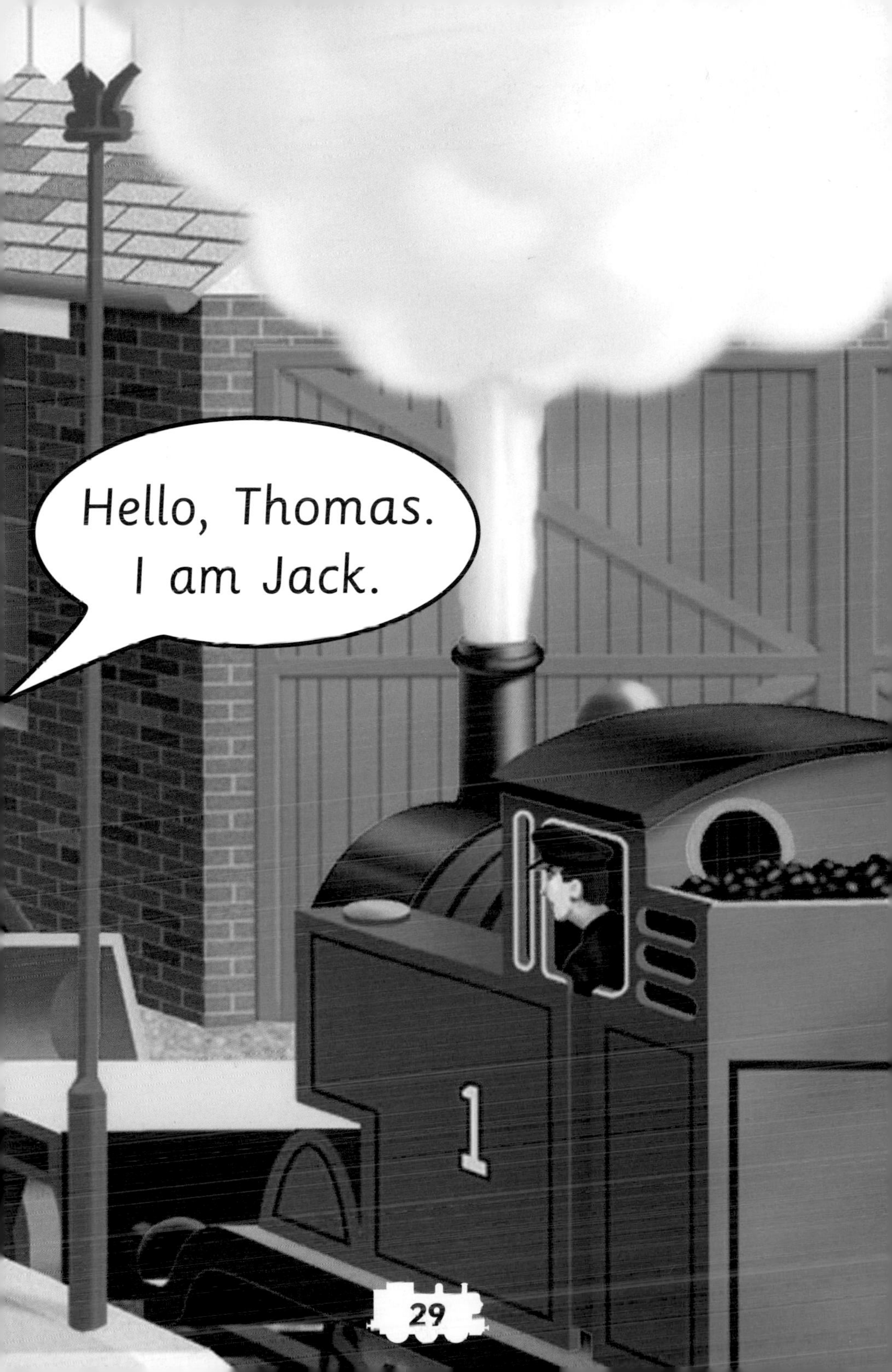
Hello, Thomas. I am Jack.

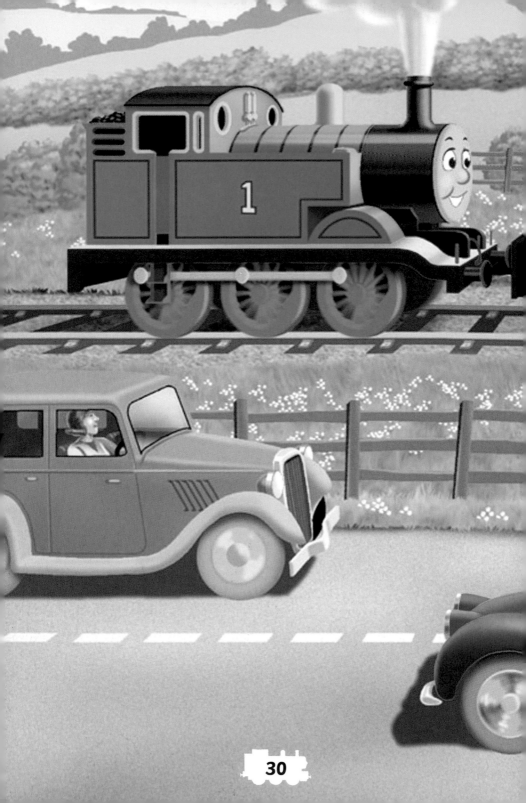

Push. Push. Jack went with Thomas.

Hello,
I am Jack. Can
I help dig?

Jack dug and
Jack did jobs.

But then, bump went Ned.

I can help.

Jack held the bricks
up for Thomas.

Jack did a good job.

Jack can dig with us.

Dig, Dig

These two pictures of busy diggers look the same but there are five differences in the second picture.

1

Answers: Jack's number is missing and so is his lamp, Alfie's face has changed and the stones he is lifting are blue and Monty is yellow rather than red.

Read these words:

dig   rock   sand

At the Pit

In this story Bill and Ben
work at the pit.

Read these words:

hit   hat   fit

Which words rhyme with pit?